Mingxia and Chun Hua's love for nature's beauty

Jesuseme O. Oyareghan

AuthorHouse™ UK
1663 Liberty Drive
Bloomington, IN 47403 USA
www.authorhouse.co.uk
UK TFN: 0800 0148641 (Toll Free inside the UK)
UK Local: 02036 956322 (+44 20 3695 6322 from outside the UK)

This book is printed on acid-free paper.

ISBN: 979-8-8230-8758-2 (sc)
979-8-8230-8759-9 (e)

Library of Congress Control Number: 2024909806

Print information available on the last page.

Published by AuthorHouse 08/08/2024

authorHOUSE®

Dedication

To the glory of God. This book is dedicated to my dad and mom for their support through the publication process and to everybody that values friends and friendship.

Table of Contents

Chapter 1

The Red Panda Forest

Once upon a time, there was a village in the middle of a bamboo forest in China. This village was named after the Great Wall of China which gave it, the name Jingzhu. This name is because the Great Wall of China was built over many cities with bamboo forests.

This bamboo forest got a nickname called the red panda forest. This was because this forest was once inhabited by billions of red pandas but China was now developing and people had come to destroy the middle of the bamboo forest. After it had been cut down thousands of red pandas died because they got their energy from the middle part of the forest.

Chapter 2

The Pandas Revenge

The pandas got angry and decided to talk to the people to stop destroying the forest but they ignored the pandas and calamity fell, the pandas constructed a temple to their honor using their power and then placed a curse that whoever stepped foot close to the forbidden gate without a clean heart would die and if the two friends do not save the bamboo forest and the red pandas in twenty years the pandas would release their wrath and let all the red pandas out in the whole of china. Therefore, people died and it became a wasteland until the Jingzhu village started to grow and brought it to life again.

The temple

Chapter 3

The Forbidden Gate and its Legend

In the depths of the bamboo forest lies a forbidden gate, where the red panda spirit and its descendants live. Legends speak of two friends with pure hearts who will face many challenges and even be separated, but their love for nature will save the forest. When they finally realize their duty, a golden light will shine over the bamboo forest like never before.

In Jingzhu village there was an ancient temple named the panda temple because of the love the locals had for the pandas and beside it was two huts. In these huts there lived the Jinxiu family and the Rosemallow family, the Jinxiu family had a daughter named Mingxia, and the Rosemallows had a daughter named Chun Hua.

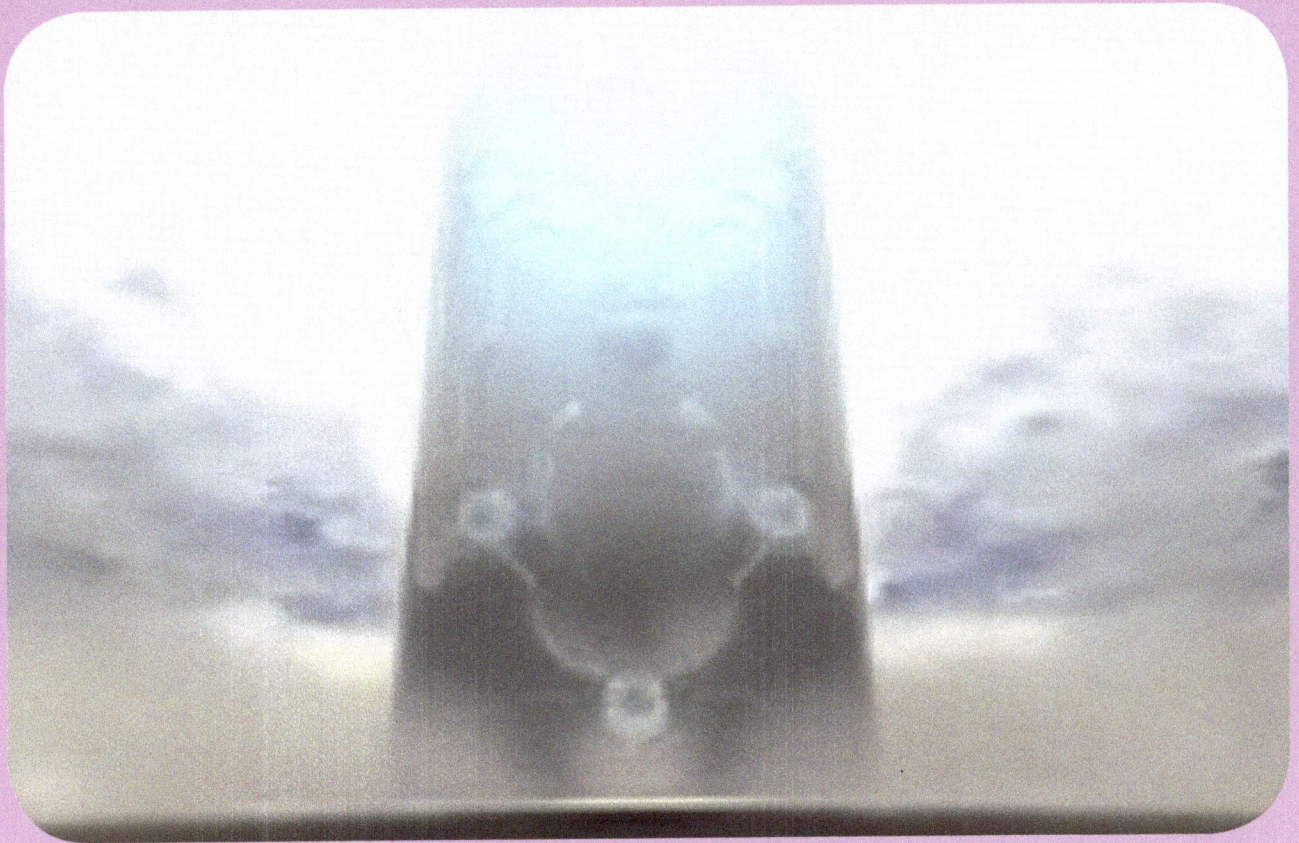

the forbidden gate

Chapter 4

Formal Rivals

The parents of Mingxia and Chun Hua were formal friends but when they both got the title of Chiefs, they wanted to prove to each other that they were superior, which is why they wanted to become the king's adviser. Therefore, the hatred which drove them to be rivals was because they were high chiefs in the village which is why their huts are built beside the temple and this anger made the families separated their children.

In mingxia and chun hua eyes, nature beauty shines bright

Mingxia and Chun Hua

Though, the families were rivals the girls were still friends and this friendship was kindled by their undying love for the bamboo forest and the animals in it. Their love for nature was so strong that every day the girls secretly went to the forest to listen to the rustling of the bamboo leaves, they loved to hear the stream and the birds sing early in the morning, they loved twittering, tweeting and chirps of the wild birds and also loved to see the moist on the bright green leaves of the bamboo. They loved to get the fresh green, grassy straw-like scent spread by the wind. The girl's favourite animals in the forest are pandas.

Chapter 5

Different Personalities

Though they both loved nature they had very different personalities, Mingxia was a girl of culture and her language, she loved to study their myths and legends, while Chun Hua was a smart curious girl who loved the outdoors and exploring the forests, she was never interested in her culture or her language. This caused lots of confusion and arguments between the girls and made them almost end their friendship.

This continued for years but when Mingxia's parents found out about their daughter being friends with Chun Hua, they got furious and waited for Chun Hua's eighth birthday. It was their way of getting back at Chun Hua's family. They planned to get rid of Chun Hua by sending her to the thickest part of the forest where the legendary red panda spirit and its descendants lived.

Chapter 6

The Trials

This part of the bamboo forest was forbidden for the villagers cause of the legend of the forbidden gate, only the two friends with the purest hearts would be able to pass the forbidden gate without being killed or quit their journey.

Unknowingly for Mingxia's parents Chun Hua and Mingxia were the two friends with pure hearts. On Chun Hua's way to the forbidden gate, she encountered a devastating situation where she saw people cutting down the bamboo trees, she was so angry but she saw the type of tools they had and she taught she could not defeat them but her love for nature was too strong therefore she could not bear to see the forest in pain luckily her curiosity helped her out and she was able to communicate with the animals in the forest they helped her by creating a song completely out of harmony.

Chapter 7

Strange Creatures Arise

This angered the forest cutters and they left.

She continued her journey to the forbidden gate on her way she was attacked by a bunch of unknown animals that made strange noises she tried to fight against these animals that looked like legendary creatures, for example, the Bashe a python-like snake that ate elephants, Bixi, a dragon with the shell of a turtle, Black Tortoise, a turtle that represents the cardinal point North and Winter and Baku a tapir-like creature that lives by eating people's dreams.

She then understood what she had to do to get rid of these legendary yet mythical creatures and was successful, she then learned that to survive out in this unknown part of the forest she had to use her knowledge and understanding she will also have to be one with nature.

bashe

bixi

Chapter 8

Lost in the forest

Back in Jingzhu village Mingxia was worried about not seeing her friend for a long time she then decided to ask her parents but on her way, she heard her parents discussing how they had sent her friend to the forbidden gate with the intention of her getting killed, she cried as she heard that, just then her parents saw her crying and immediately knew she had heard them but before they could stop her she had run away into the bamboo forest talking to herself about how despicable her parents were.

She was so busy sobbing to herself that she got lost in the thick bamboo forest, after some time she got seriously tired and decided to take a nap while taking a nap a baby red panda suddenly came beside her rubbing itself against her leg startling her and making her jump back to her feet when she saw the baby red panda she was shocked cause only when the legend is fulfilled can the red pandas come out through the forbidden gate.

Red

Chapter 9

The Encounter with the Red Pandas

She pushes her thoughts aside, takes the baby panda with her, names it Red, and continues the journey. Meanwhile, Chun Hua has been able to defeat the strange animals she also learned that the only way to defeat the animals and overcome the trials is to adapt to the situation and learn more about her culture and legends, putting this knowledge together, therefore, she continued her journey looking for shelter, she finally found her way to a cave, where she decided to take a rest but when she entered the cave she found a red panda in the cave that had been sleeping and named it Dozer she decided to take the panda with her so that it could sleep in her warmth.

Dozer

Chapter 10

When it is Right

After waking up, Mingxia found out that she had overslept. She saw Red chewing a bamboo stem, picked up the small panda, and kept going forward without knowing what lay ahead of her. Suddenly she hears a tiny voice saying hi, she tries looking for where it came from but is not able to find who said it. She suddenly heard the voice again saying, "Hi, it's me red." The little voice said; she was so startled. She nearly dropped the baby panda to the ground.

In shock, she asked the baby panda what it was doing outside the forbidden gate, the little panda told her that it had been sent by the legendary panda spirit to help the forest saviours out with their trials, she was surprised and asked the baby panda if it could tell her who the saviours were, the little creature refuses and says she will know when it is time.

Chapter 11

In the middle of the Forest

Though she did not understand what the panda meant by that her thoughts were soon interrupted by the panda telling her that he would guide her to safety, he then started to tell her how he got lost cause it was his first time out of the forbidden gate and he is still new to the bamboo forest and its wide and dense surroundings making it hard to move in the forest.

She followed the creature's advice until they were in the middle of the bamboo forest she was so surprised she was able to get to the middle of the bamboo forest without getting injured, suddenly she heard sets of strange noises coming from behind her that she had never heard before these noises included noises resembling screams and roars echoing through the forest, she was so afraid that she tried to run away but the noises kept on coming closer and closer so she decided to face these creatures.

Chapter 12

Observation is the Key

She quickly put her knowledge to use and observed these animals made the same noises as some legendary creatures and looked like these legendary creatures, for example, the Bashe a python-like snake that ate elephants, Bixi, a dragon with the shell of a turtle, Black Tortoise, a turtle that represents the cardinal point North and Winter and Baku a tapir-like creature that lives by eating people›s dreams, seeing all these she still wanted to test these creatures to see if they are from the legends but before she could act little red gave her some advice ‹›look closely the truth can be covered but their deceit is strong››.

Chapter 13

Advice

She kept thinking of what Little Red had said and decided to study each of their weaknesses and relate it to each of the legendary creatures they look like and find out how similar they are to each legendary creature, she started with Bashe and as they continued to fight she discovered his weakness was self-content, Bixi›s weakness was acting weak cause of his sympathy, Black Tortoise was said to be a warrior and a symbol of eternity and Baku›s weakness is not having hope›s or dreams.

After a while, she puts it all together and finds a way to defeat these beasts. After lots of fighting Little Red secretly channels strength to her to keep fighting, after hours of fighting, she is able to defeat all the legendary creatures of China. Just then the advice Little Red gave her came rushing back into her memory making her happy. She then said to herself, "Now I know that teamwork, observation, patience and advice are the key to survival."

Chapter 14

Cry for help

Meanwhile, in Jingzhu village, Mingzia's parents had confessed their bad deed but because of the rumours of the death of people without pure hearts the villagers refused to help the families which made the two families cry, they then decided that they would set their differences apart and go to the bamboo forest together in search of their daughters, but before they could step foot in the bamboo forest there was a sudden golden shinning dome surrounding the forest and keeping the village in the middle.

The parents were so sad cause their kids were stuck in the bamboo forest filled with legendary creatures. Meanwhile,

Chun Hua was looking for her way to the forbidden gate with dozer, suddenly dozer started talking to her and she was surprised she asked him how he escaped the forbidden gate but the little dozer told her that he would take her to the forbidden gate and she obeyed the little one's advice.

The golden dome

Chapter 15

The Forbidden Gate is not found

Chun Hua and Mingxia had now met in the Middle of the forest where there is said to be a forbidden gate to the red panda spirit world. When they both saw each other they cried tears of joy and happiness, but their happiness was cut short by Red and Dozer.

They suddenly realized they were in the middle of the bamboo forest, they both looked at each other curiously wandering where the forbidden gate was but when they asked their baby red pandas the pandas echoed "the saviours will have to say the magic word together for the gate to be revealed".

Chapter 16

The Crisis

The girls looked at each other as if silently wondering what the magic word could be. Suddenly both girls said "Harmony and friendship between humans and nature" and the forbidden gate was revealed. It opened with a burst of wind sweeping the fragrance of the bamboo forest with it and millions of red pandas were released into the bamboo forest.

Just then a gust of wind lifted the girls into the air they all of a sudden could talk to the red pandas as if they had been the ones to create these beautiful creatures and for once in a long time they felt very happy. Meanwhile, in Jingzhu the wind was felt and everyone was surprised cause they had never felt such a strong wind before, some villagers even assumed that the two girls and her parents had angered the legendary red panda spirit and were even persisting on killing the parents.

Chapter 17

The Guardians

The next day the two friends wanted to go back home but were immediately stopped by Red and Dozer saying they wanted to come with them, the friends agreed and the little red pandas followed, on their way home the girls asked why the red pandas did not tell them they were the saviours the red pandas told her them that it was forbidden and it would cause havoc and their duties as their guardian red pandas. When they got to Jigzhu village the villagers were surprised to see the girls back from the forbidden gate but were even more surprised when they brought back home red pandas.

Chapter 18

The Legend is Fulfilled

The girls excitedly shared their encounters with red pandas, how they became legendary saviours, and how the red panda spirit made peace with humans to break the curse. They also educated the villagers about the bamboo forest's importance and inhabitants.

The girl's parents were proud and a story about their happiness continued for years.

Conclusion

Friendship is a strong bond and is to be valued, teamwork, advice and observation were the key to success in this story and nature should always be valued

www.ingramcontent.com/pod-product-compliance
Ingram Content Group UK Ltd.
Pitfield, Milton Keynes, MK11 3LW, UK
UKHW050735030125
452892UK00013B/83